How Do They Grow?

From Piglet to Pig

by Jillian Powell

RAINTREE
STECK-VAUGHN
PUBLISHERS

A Harcourt Company

Austin   New York
www.raintreesteckvaughn.com

Published by Raintree Steck-Vaughn Publishers, an imprint of Steck-Vaughn Company

Library of Congress Cataloging-in-Publication Data

Powell, Jillian.
   From piglet to pig / by Jillian Powell.
    p. cm.-- (How do they grow?)
   Includes bibliographical references (p.).
   ISBN 0-7398-4428-8
    1. Piglets--Juvenile literature. 2. Swine--Development--Juvenile literature. [1. Pigs. 2. Animals--Infancy.] I. Title.

SF395.5 .P68 2001
636.4'07--dc21   2001019336

Printed in Italy. Bound in the United States.
1 2 3 4 5 6 7 8 9 0 LB 05 04 03 02 01

Picture acknowledgments
Agripicture 18 (Peter Dean); Angela Hampton Family Life Photolibrary 10, 13, 17, 23, 24, 27; Ecoscene 8 (David Wootton); Ole Steen Hansen 9, 19, 20, 29; Holt Studios International 6 (Gordon Roberts), 7 (William Harinck), 12 (William Harinck), 16 (David Burton), 21 (Nigel Cattlin); NHPA title page; 4 (E.A. Janes); HWPL 5, 11, 22, 25; Oxford Scientific Films 26 (Michael Leach); RSPCA 4 (Andrew Linscott), 14 (Andrew Linscott), 15 (Andrew Linscott), 28 (J.B. Blossom).

Contents

Words in **bold** in the text can be found in the glossary on page 30.

Making a Nest

The **sows** on this pig farm live outdoors. They sleep in huts called **hoop shelters**. Some of the sows are **pregnant** and will soon have piglets.

This sow is getting ready to have piglets. She makes a nest of straw. The nest will keep her piglets warm when they are born.

Newborn Piglets

The sow has had a **litter** of 11 piglets.
She is tired now. She sleeps while the
piglets drink her milk.

These young piglets are resting. Their coats are thin and damp. The lamp is keeping them warm.

Young Piglets

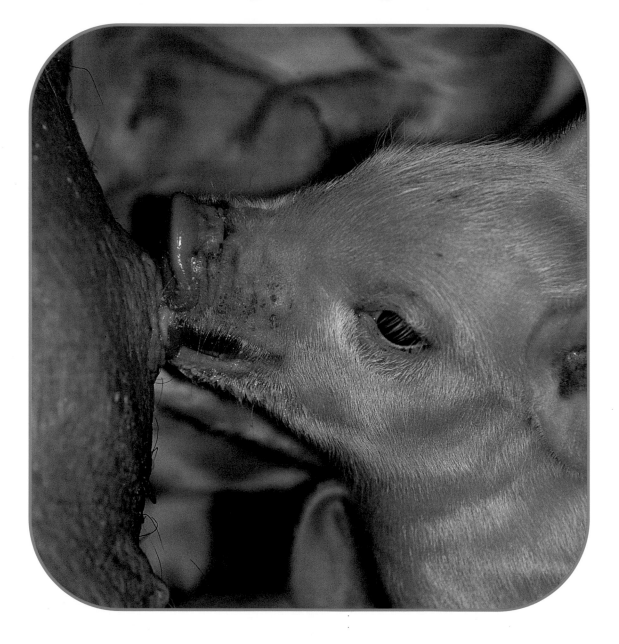

The piglets drink their mother's milk for the first few weeks of their lives. The milk helps them to grow strong and fight off **germs**.

This piglet likes to play. Piglets are clever animals, and they learn quickly.
They like to explore the world around them.

Getting Stronger

These piglets are a few days old. Their long curly tails are cut shorter to stop other piglets from biting them. This is called **docking**.

The piglets are also given a **shot** of **iron**. This keeps them strong and healthy.

Feeding and Growing

When they are a week old, the piglets start to eat dry food made from milk. This will help them to grow fast. At about five weeks they are **weaned**.

This piglet now weighs about 15 pounds (7 kg). This is five times more than when the piglet was born.

Growing Together

The piglets now live together in a weaning pen.
They sleep on straw and eat their food from a
feeding **trough**.

All the piglets have a **tag** put in one ear.
The tags have numbers so
the farm workers can
tell the piglets apart.

Exploring Outdoors

These piglets are growing up on an outdoor pig farm. They can run around in the field and search for food.

The sow uses her snout to sniff out **roots** in the ground to eat. This piglet is copying its mother. Pigs and piglets have a very good sense of smell.

Keeping Warm or Cool

When it is cold in winter, the shelters keep the piglets warm and dry. Their thin coats mean that they can easily feel the heat or cold.

When it is hot in summer, the pigs and piglets like to roll in the mud. This helps them to stay cool.

The farm worker feeds the piglets on **pellets** of grower food. These help them to grow quickly. Every 2 pounds (1 kg) of food they eat makes them grow 7 pounds (3 kg) heavier.

The piglets need plenty of fresh water every day.
They drink from a water trough in their field.

Keeping Healthy

On some pig farms, the piglets grow up indoors. The farm worker makes sure the straw in the pig shed is clean and dry. This way the piglets will stay healthy.

If any of the piglets is sick or hurt, the farmer sends for the vet. The vet may give the piglet some **medicine** to make it better.

Ready to Be Sold

The farm worker is weighing this piglet to see how heavy it is. When the piglets weigh about 220 pounds (100 kg), they are ready to be sold.

These piglets are six months old and they are ready to be sold for meat. The farm worker loads them onto a truck to go to the market.

Boars and Sows

The farmer keeps a **boar** to **mate** with the sows.
After they have mated, some of the sows
will have piglets growing inside them.

This sow is pregnant. The **ultrasound** machine tells the farm worker that there are baby piglets growing inside the sow.

Having Piglets

The piglets grow inside the sow for 16 weeks.
A sow may have two or three litters in a year.

This sow has had a litter of piglets. She will feed them and look after them. This way they will grow up to be strong, healthy pigs.

29

Glossary

Boar (bor) A male pig.

Docking (DOK-ing) Making an animal's tail shorter.

Germs (jurmz) Tiny particles around us that can carry diseases.

Hoop Shelters (hoop SHEL-turz) Huts where pigs sleep on an outdoor pig farm.

Iron (EYE-urn) A mineral that helps keep the blood healthy.

Litter (LIT-ur) All the young animals born to the same mother at the same time.

Mate When a male and female come together to have babies.

Medicine (MED-uh-suhn) Drugs that are taken to avoid illness or disease.

Pellets (PEL-lits) Small, round pieces of food.

Pregnant (PREG-nuhnt) When a female has young growing inside her.

Roots The parts of a plant that grow underground.

Shot Giving an animal medicine using a needle.

Sows (sous) Female pigs.

Tag A label that shows the name or number of something.

Trough (trawf) A long container that holds food or water for farm animals.

Ultrasound (UHL-truh-sound) A machine helps the farmer hear the heartbeats of babies growing inside their mother.

Weaned (weend) When a young animal stops drinking its mother's milk.

Further Information

Books

Gibbons, Gail. *Pigs*. Holiday, 1988.

King-Smith, Dick. *All Pigs are Beautiful*.
(Read & Wonder Books). Candlewick
Press, 1995.

Most, Bernard. *Oink-Ha!*. Harcourt, 1997.

Munsch, Robert. *Pigs*. Firefly Books
Limited, 1989.

Spencer, Eve. *Animal Babies One Two
Three*. (Ready-Set-Read series). Raintree
Steck–Vaughn, 1990.

Stone, Lynn M. *Pigs* (Farm Animals
Discovery Library series). Rourke
Corporation, 1990.

Video

Farm Animals narrated by Johnny Morris
(Dorling Kindersley)

On the Farm: Baby Animals (Dorling
Kindersley)

Lets Go to the Farm/Baby Animals
(Countryside Products). Visit their website
at: **www.countrysidevideos.com**

Websites

www.pbs.org/wnet/nature/pigs/
Discover the truth about pigs. Find out how
some pigs have moved out of the barn and
into the house. Learn about the many
different types of pigs all around the world.

www.pigs.org/
For the past four years, this organization
has helped to find homes for thousands of
pigs.

www.pigspeace.org/
Since 1994, this organization has given
pigs medical care, a healthy diet, and a
real home.

www.ics.uci.edu/~pazzani/4H/pigs.html
This goal of this project is to communicate
through activities such as shows, talks,
contests, tours, and exhibits.

Useful addresses

National 4-H Council
7100 CT Avenue
Chevy Chase, MD 20815
Phone: (301) 961-2800

Index